D0004676

Kaylee Finds a Friend

Kaylee

Enjoy the
Story about
Friendship!
Warmly,
Kim Roderiques

by Anne D. LeClaire

photography by Kim Roderiques

-Charlie

This book is dedicated to all children
looking for their very special friend.

Published by Golden Paws Publishing

Copyright 2018 by Golden Paws Publishing
All rights reserved.
Published 2018.

ISBN 978-0-9978182-8-4

www.goldenpawspublishing.com

Special thanks to Marcy Ford for her nature photography (pages 3, 4, 33, and 35 (squirrel).

Thank you to artists Tatutina (page 13) and Ronni Reasonover (page 35).

This book was designed and typeset by Nancy Viall Shoemaker of West Barnstable Press, West Barnstable, MA. www.westbarnstablepress.com
The fonts used are Myriad Pro and Good Dog, a typeface appropriately named for use in this book. Good Dog was designed by Ethan Dunham in 1996.
Myriad was created by Robert Slimbach and Carol Twombly for Adobe in 1992.
Kaylee Finds a Friend was printed in the USA on 100 lb. white matte coated.

Kaylee finds a friend   1

On Monday morning, Kaylee woke up and looked out her window at the blue and cloudless sky.

"Today," she said, "is a perfect day to find a friend."

After breakfast, Kaylee sat on the steps of her front porch and looked down the street.

At that moment, a cardinal landed on the bush next to the bottom step. It looked right at her and sang its cardinal song. Cheer-cheer-cheer.

"Today," Kaylee said to the bright red bird, "Today is a perfect day to find a friend."

The cardinal chirped and flew away.

Next, a monarch flitted by and flew to the row of zinnias Kaylee's mother had planted by the fence. It landed on a pink blossom.

"Today," Kaylee said to the butterfly, "is a perfect day to find a special friend."

The monarch fluttered its orange and black wings and then it flew away.

A few minutes later, Charlie, the golden retriever who lived in the house next door, wandered over.

"Hi, Charlie," Kaylee said. "Today I am going to find a very special friend."

Charlie tilted his head. "Arf," he barked, as if to say, "Where would you go to find a very special friend?"

"I think I will find my very special friend at the beach," Kaylee said. "Do you want to come, too?"

Charlie wagged his tail and together they headed off to the beach.

When they got to the beach Charlie ran ahead across the sand. A moment later he came back carrying an old blue shoe in his mouth.

He dropped it at her feet.

"Oh, Charlie," Kaylee laughed. She knew Charlie was a retriever and retrievers like to fetch things.

Then Charlie found a clam shell. He began to chew it, because retrievers like to chew things, too.

"Oh, no, Charlie," Kaylee said. "You cannot eat a shell. It will make you sick."

Next Charlie found a yellow ball.

Kaylee threw the ball and Charlie chased it and brought it back to her. Over and over. Because golden retrievers never get tired of a game of retrieving.

After a while they headed home.

They had found a blue shoe, a clam shell, and a yellow ball.

But Kaylee had not found a very special friend.

On Tuesday morning, Kaylee woke up and looked out the window and saw fat, fluffy clouds in the sky. Her Daddy had told her these were cumulus clouds and meant there would be good weather.

Today, she thought, would be a fine day to walk in the park. Perhaps she would find a very special friend there.

As she passed Charlie's house, he ran over to her and wagged his tail.

"Okay, Charlie," Kaylee said. "You can come, too."

When they got to the park, they saw a special exhibit. It was called Sharks in the Park. They were not real sharks. They were made of wood.

Some were painted in bright colors.

Some were decorated with glass and beads.

They met a white poodle. They saw a fat gray squirrel.

Charlie did not bark at the poodle.

He did not chase the gray squirrel.

"Good boy," Kaylee said.

After a while, they headed home.

They had seen
      twenty decorated sharks,
         a white poodle,
            and a fat gray squirrel.

But Kaylee had not found a very special friend.

When Kaylee woke up on Wednesday morning and looked out the window, she saw the leaves on a tree blowing in the wind.

"Today," she said, "I hope I find a very special friend."

She remembered that her mother made lists of things because she said it was important to be organized. "Today is a good day to get organized," Kaylee said.

After breakfast, she went outside and sat in her favorite spot to make a list of all the things she wanted to do with her very special friend.

She had just started when Charlie wandered over.

"Hi, Charlie," she said. She told him she was getting organized.

Charlie sat down. He was very quiet while Kaylee thought and thought and wrote her list.

This is Kaylee's list.

Things I will do with a very special friend:
1. Walk in the park.
2. Go to the beach.
3. Eat Ice cream.
4. Have adventures.
5. Go shopping.
6. Sit and talk.
7. Read a book.

When she was done, she read the list to Charlie.

He listened very carefully.

Kaylee looked at her list. She had already been to the beach and to the park and had not found a very special friend there.

"Maybe I will find a very special friend at the ice cream store," she said.

Of course, Charlie wanted to go, too.

They got a small dish of strawberry ice cream to share. Charlie ate most of it.

"Oh, Charlie," Kaylee said. "You like ice cream even more than I do."

They finished the ice cream and then they walked home.

Kaylee did not find a very special friend on Wednesday.

On Thursday, when Kaylee woke up, she checked the list of things she would do with a very special friend.

"This is a great day for an adventure," she said. "Maybe I will find my very special friend today."

Charlie was waiting for her and together they went to the fish pier to watch the fishing boats come in and the fishermen unload their catch.

They saw lots and lots of fish.

They saw a short boy with a big green hat.

They saw a tall boy with a little orange hat.

They saw a gray seal.

But Kaylee did not find a very special friend.

On Friday, when Kaylee woke up she was feeling quiet. "Today is a perfect day to read a book," she said.

Kaylee liked to read a book just as much as Charlie liked to retrieve things – and eat ice cream.

She had just settled down with her book when Charlie came over. He tilted his head as if to say, "What are we going to do today?"

"I will read you a story," she said.

Charlie listened as if he understood every word.

But when she went to bed on Friday night, Kaylee still had not found a very special friend.

On Saturday, Kaylee decided to go shopping. Perhaps she would find a very special friend at the clothing store.

"Come on, Charlie," she said, when she walked by his house. "Let's go shopping."

When they got to the store, they saw Kaylee's older friend Grace.

Together the girls looked at clothes.

Kaylee and Grace saw many pretty t-shirts and dresses.

Charlie found a perfect hat to wear to the beach.

But Kaylee did not find a very special friend.

That night, before she fell asleep, she said to her mother, "Maybe tomorrow I will find a very special friend."

"What is a very special friend?" her mother asked.

Kaylee thought for a minute.

"A very special friend is someone who is always happy to see you." she said. "They care."

"And they will listen, because sometimes you just want to talk."

Kaylee thought some more.

"And if you want to be quiet, they will understand and they will be quiet, too."

"And it's okay with them if you are feeling quiet," Kaylee said.
            Or sad.
                        Or silly."

"Because a special friend likes you just the way you are."

On Sunday morning after breakfast, Kaylee sat on the porch steps.

The cardinal came and landed on the bush next to her.

"All week I have been looking for a very special friend," Kaylee told the bright red bird.

Then the butterfly with orange and black wings flew by and landed on a flower right next to Kaylee.

Kaylee sat very still so the butterfly and the bird wouldn't fly away. She told them about her week.

"I looked for someone to play with and have adventures with and to talk with. Someone to go with me to the beach and to the park," she said.

"I looked and looked but I didn't find a very special friend."

Just then Charlie came over. He was so happy to see her. He wagged his doggy tail and grinned his big doggy smile. He waited to see what they would do today.

"Oh, Charlie," Kaylee said. "What a good time we had while we were looking for a very special friend."

She thought about the gray seal they had seen at the fish pier. And the short boy with the big green hat. And the tall boy with the little orange one. She thought about the day they went shopping and how funny Charlie looked in his hat.

She remembered the morning they spent at the beach and the old blue shoe Charlie brought to her. She thought about the game of toss and retrieve they had played. Over and over.

She remembered the dish of strawberry ice cream they had shared (even though Charlie had eaten most of it).

She thought about the white poodle and fat gray squirrel and the twenty wooden sharks they had seen in the park.

Kaylee thought about all the fun they'd had all week and then jumped right up off the step.

"Oh, Charlie," she said. "It's you." She gave him a great big hug.

Charlie looked at her with his brown retriever eyes and wagged his tail.

"It's you," Kaylee said again. "You are my very special friend."

"Arf," Charlie barked, as if to say, "Sometimes a very special friend is there all along, just waiting for you to see him."

Our wish is
for everyone
to find
a very
special friend.

All of Kaylee's clothing provided by Chatham Kids of Chatham, Massachusetts.